MACARONI
The Purple Pony

Created and Written by:
Felicia Ann Clements

Illustrations by:
Chris Herrick

To Kaitlyn
Felicia A. Clements
09·28·2011

First published in 2010.

Printed in the United States of America.

First Edition

Manufacturing by CreateSpace

Book design by Felicia Ann Clements

www.macaronithepurplepony.com

ISBN-13: 978-1456555155 (CreateSpace Assigned)
ISBN-10: 14565551111
BISAC: JUV057000 JUVENILE FICTION / Stories in Verse

This book is dedicated to the memory of my mother Susan D. Bagdade who was truly the greatest mother a daughter could ever wish for.

Macaroni the purple pony was born on an August day, and much to his dismay, he cried, "I'm not black or brown or grey!"

"Oh no!" he screamed, "this is utterly absurd!
Surely I'll be laughed at by others in the herd!"

"What can I do," he said,
"except for run and hide?
Maybe there's a purple herd
up on the other side."

So off he went all by himself to search for his own kind,
wandering out in the world not knowing what he'd find.

He walked and searched for miles and miles and for many tiring days, hoping to discover where all the purple ponies graze.

He missed his land and family and wished he could go home
Maybe they would love him and he could end his fruitless

Of course his pony parents would be looking for him soon.
"I know they'll understand if I march to a different tune."

Very soon thereafter, the purple pony foal was found,
galloping through the hills and after searching all around.

Mama Mare and Papa Stallion had to find their baby pony,
the beloved purple pony son they'd proudly named "Macaroni."

Tired and discouraged, Macaroni headed back.
With Ma and Pa beside him, confidence he did not lack.

"My Mama and my Papa wondered why I ran away,
but I was so ashamed, I did not know just what to say."

Then he blurted out, "I'm so different from all the rest!"
but Papa Stallion said, "That doesn't mean you're second best!

"I think you are mistaken and completely unaware.
Your color is original, beautiful and rare!"

So Papa said, "Stand up tall and prance and neigh and dance.
My little Macaroni son, please give yourself a chance."

When they finally arrived back home unto their loving herd,
he could not believe his eyes, and he became so self-assured.

His Mama and his Papa said, "Come meet our neighbor, Lily."
To his surprise, there stood before him the cutest pinkish filly.

Then they trotted past the knoll to see a gorgeous mare,
a vision in the color blue named "Famous Foxy Blair."

One more stop across the stream to see a colt named Joe.
In his full-length yellow jacket, he was putting on a show.

"The lesson that I learned," he said, "is my color's part of me. In all my purple glory, I just have to let it be."

ACKNOWLEDGEMENTS

I would like to thank the following people for their support:

My incredible husband, Bill Clements, is my honest "sounding board" for all of my work, and he contributed greatly to this project.

My father, Dr. Allen D. Bagdade, provided unconditional devotion and amazingly fun ideas. My brother, David Bagdade, was instrumental in getting Macaroni off the ground.

I owe a tremendous debt of gratitude to the greatest agent in the world, Anson Sims of A. Sims Associates, who has been an invaluable resource.

Thank you to Chris Herrick, Macaroni's gifted illustrator; Jacob Nicholas and Sona Jacob of Sona & Jacob Studios, whose artistic skills helped bring Macaroni and his friends to life; to Ellen Green for her inspiring pre-illustration work; to Sue Klein for her positive energy and input; and to Kay Dean for reviewing my material with a teacher's mind and offering constructive suggestions.

Macaroni the Purple Pony is the first book in a series of five. The next book to follow, A Winning Color, will be coming soon.

Made in the USA
Charleston, SC
12 April 2011